A Tintin Film Book

TINTIN
AND THE
LAKE
OF
SHARKS

Based on the characters created by Hergé

Translated by Leslie Lonsdale-Cooper
and Michael Turner

Artwork copyright © 1973 by Éditions Casterman, Tournai.
Library of Congress Catalogue Card Number Afo 72745
Text © 1973 by Egmont Children's Books Ltd.
First published in Great Britain in 1973.
Published as a paperback in 1975
Reprinted 1977
Reprinted as a Magnet paperback 1978.
Reprinted eight times.
Reissued 1990 by Mammoth,
an imprint of Egmont Children's Books Limited
239 Kensington High Street, London W8 6SL

Reprinted 1991 (twice), 1993 (twice) 1994, 1995, 1996, 1997, 1998 , 1999 , 2001

Printed in Belgium by Casterman Printers s.a., Tournai
ISBN 0-7497-0365-2

Lamplight gleams on the rain-washed streets. All is quiet: the city sleeps. Only a car moves in the night, creeping silently into the square...

...stopping in front of the Museum of Oceanography. Two men get out ...

MUSEUM OF OCEANO

...and slip cautiously into a narrow alley beside the building.

Any good, Joe?

Do it in my sleep, Harry boy! Cut a circle in the glass, shove a hand through... and bob's your uncle!

Come on! This is the place. It's that way ...

Oh, brother!... What a beaut! The biggest pearl in the world!

No problem to break into the showcase, lift the marvellous jewel from its shell ... Then, suddenly ...

Lights! ... A guard on his rounds!... Get out of sight, quick!

Look at the pearl! ... It's gone!...

STOP THIEF!

Despite the warning the travellers climb into the cart and set off with the children towards the Villa Sprog... But, high on a cliff, someone is watching them... Their pilot!

Vulture Four calling Neptune... Operation Sardine unsuccessful Customers heading for rendezvous two... Over and out!

Winding their way through the hills the travellers come at last to the Villa Sprog, built on the lakeside.

Here you are at last! I was getting quite worried!

Dear old Cuthbert! Blistering barnacles, it's good to see you!

Thank you again for everything... We'll see you tomorrow?

The Captain doesn't waste time: he heads for the bar...

I'm dry as a bone after all that cliff hanging! I need a whisky...

YOW!

Billions of bilious blue blistering barnacles... What's this?... An indoor mirage?!

The bar was just a three-dimensional image. I'm trying out this machine... I'll explain everything while we have supper. Madame Flik, my housekeeper, has prepared a special savoury szlaszek ... So come and sit down.

Now, Professor, tell us about your phantom furniture.

Certainly not...just simple diapositives. What I'm trying to create are sort of photocopies in relief.

But it's absolutely top secret...there are greedy people about...

Aha! Forgers!

What?!

What forgers?

More and more works of art are being stolen, all over the world... Thieves take an original, and leave behind a forgery...

At first, they used nothing but crude copies...

But in recent months it's taken an expert to spot the fakes, they're so good.

Anyway, Professor, let's enjoy our holiday with you, in spite of the journey!

You must be very tired. Madame Flik will show you your rooms.

Captain Haddock and the Thompsons are soon asleep, but Tintin lies awake puzzling over the day's events.

Oh well, it's no good worrying ourselves... Good night, Snowy, sleep well.

All is quiet...

...when...suddenly...

KRIIK-KRIIK

KRIIK-KRIIK

Hello!...What's that noise?... Some sort of night owl, I suppose...

But the sound is coming from the well-head, where someone is turning the handle... Madame Flik!

KRIIK-KRIIK

KRIIK-KRIIK

The bucket brings up a strange load... a walkie-talkie!

Agent Rameses calling King Shark!... Calling King Shark!...

Beside the mysterious observer two frogmen wait...

You saw them?... The one with the tuft of hair is Tintin... He is extremely dangerous! ... Operation Crab goes ahead. You have your orders. Use the new laughing gas!

Tintin returns to the Villa Sprog. Immediately Captain Haddock tells him of the morning's events. Tintin listens carefully.

Part of a flipper torn off by Snowy... The professor's lost papers... It all begins to make sense...

Now we've got this bit of rubber, perhaps the dogs can track the frogman's route...

Tintin follows Snowy, leaving the Thompsons to guard the villa. The Captain goes after Gustav, who also seems to have picked up a trail... Snowy makes the first discovery: a metal ring half buried in the ground. Tense with excitement, Tintin pulls. Slowly, quietly, a section of rock slides open, to reveal the entrance to a cave...

Great snakes! A secret passage ... with a staircase... All right, let's go!

Down the first few steps, then suddenly...

Oh!! The door's shut!... I can't get out!... But Snowy managed to escape... I'll have to go on... nothing else I can do...

THUD

At the foot of the staircase, an amazing sight greets Tintin...

What in the world?! Treasures!! Can they be... stolen from museums, like the Thompsons said?

That's up to the Syldavian police... I must find a way out...

Light!... I'm sure this cave must be connected to the lake...

Taking a deep breath, Tintin dives...

!! Help!... A wire grille!... I'm trapped!!

Tintin wrestles desperately with the metal strands, the air draining slowly from his lungs. Just in time Snowy sees bubbles on the lake surface and dives to the rescue.

At last the wires give way!

Good old Snowy! That was a near thing!

Meanwhile, at the villa...

Professor, what does your funny machine make?

Cream cake? No, it's a special paste, which I put here, with the detectives' hats there on the other side.

I switch on the current, and ... hey presto!

There! Duplicate hats! Absolutely indistinguishable...You may try them on, gentlemen.

But... I...it's all sticky ! ...

To be precise: we're all stuck up!

Yes, I'm afraid you are. I haven't yet discovered how to stabilize the reproductions, but...

...it's only a matter of days ...

B A N G

The laughing gas is working! ... Quick, grab the children and get out ... Hurry !

HA! HA!
HA!
HA!
HA!
HA!

Tintin and Snowy are on the way home...

Look ! Someone's attacking the house !

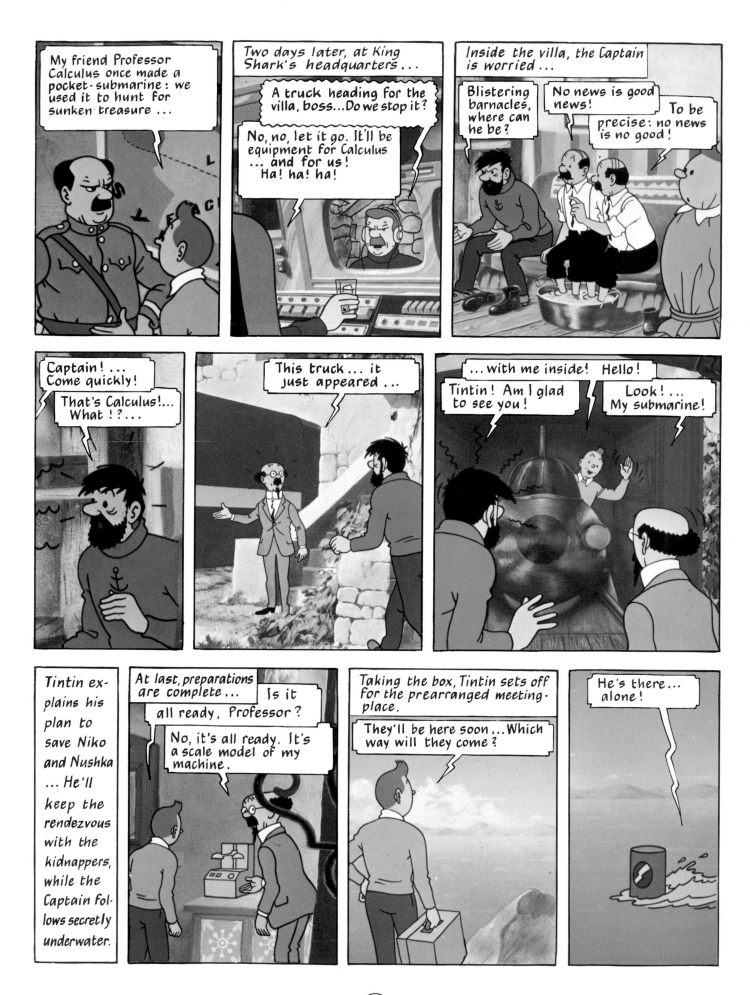

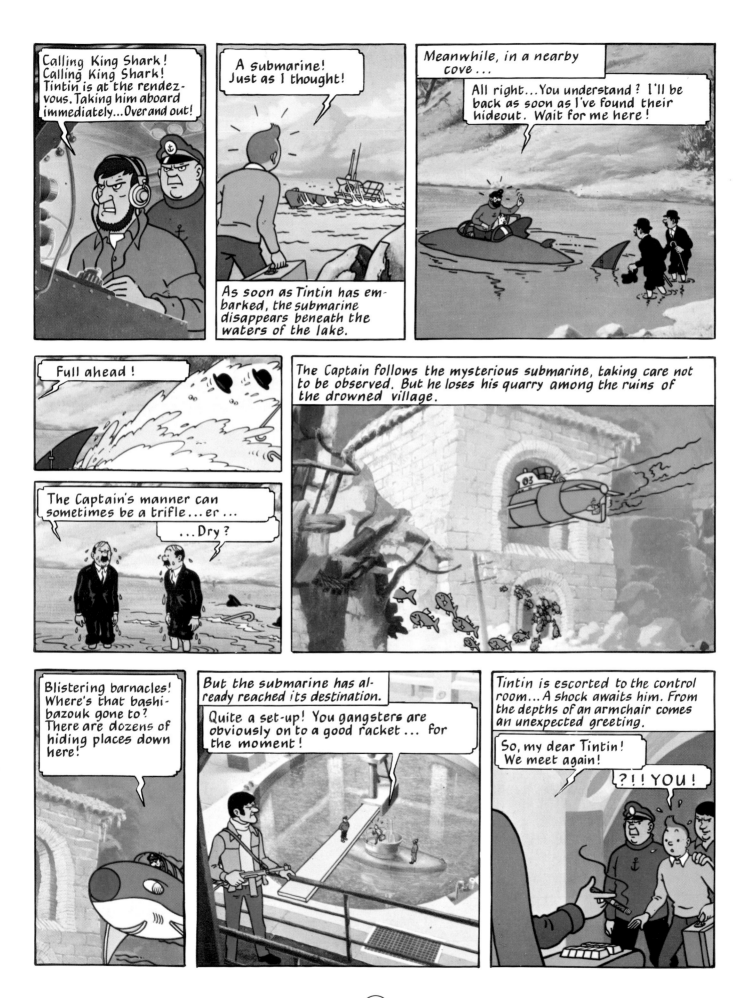

The porthole's given way! Close the watertight doors! Hurry!

With a frightening crack the glass dissolves in smithereens. The lake floods in. More by luck than judgement, Niko pilots the tank out of its dock.

Yes, boss... With the tank... through the porthole...Yes, boss... your unbreakable glass...Yes, boss ...they broke it!

You blundering fools! I'll handle this myself!... Little ruffians!

Rastapopoulos monitors the movements of the underwater tank from the control room...

Look, Nushka, we're in the old village under the lake!

What's happening? The tank won't steer any more... It's turning round...as if someone's taken control...

I'm frightened, Niko!

Ha! ha! ha! Rastapopoulos always has the last word, my little kiddywinks! ...Home you come!

Diavolo! Where did that come from?

Captain Haddock, cruising down a street, almost collides with the tank...

Road-hogs!...It's my right of way!

It's Captain Haddock!... Captain, Captain, it's us!

Aaaghrr! A couple of salvoes will settle his hash!... Four, three, two...

Stop! You can't do that!

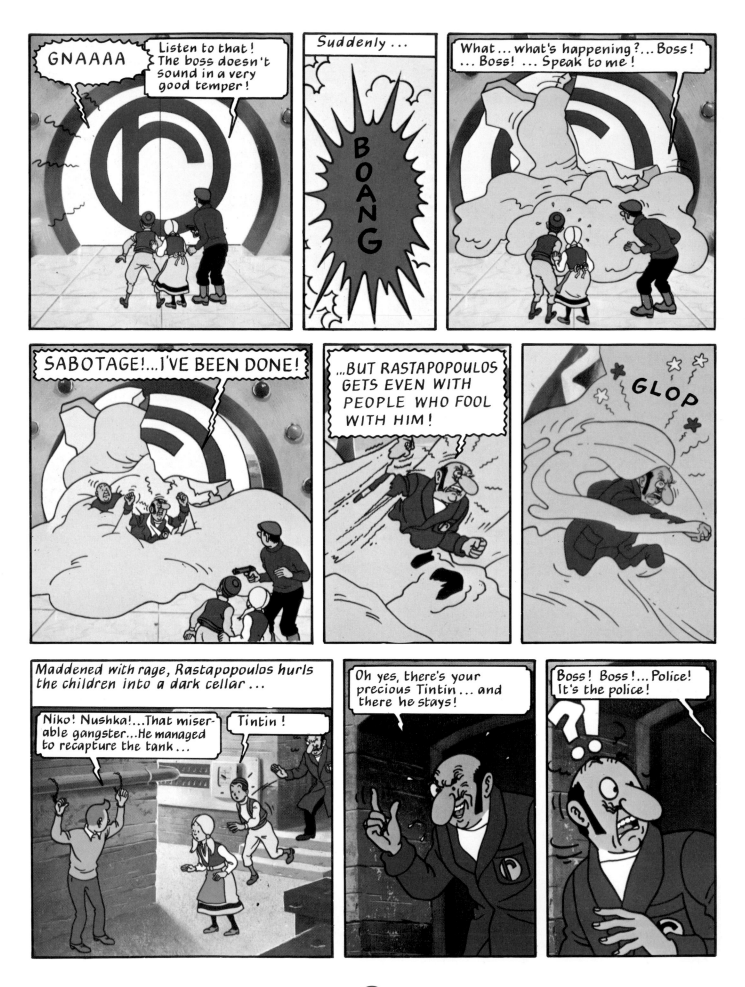

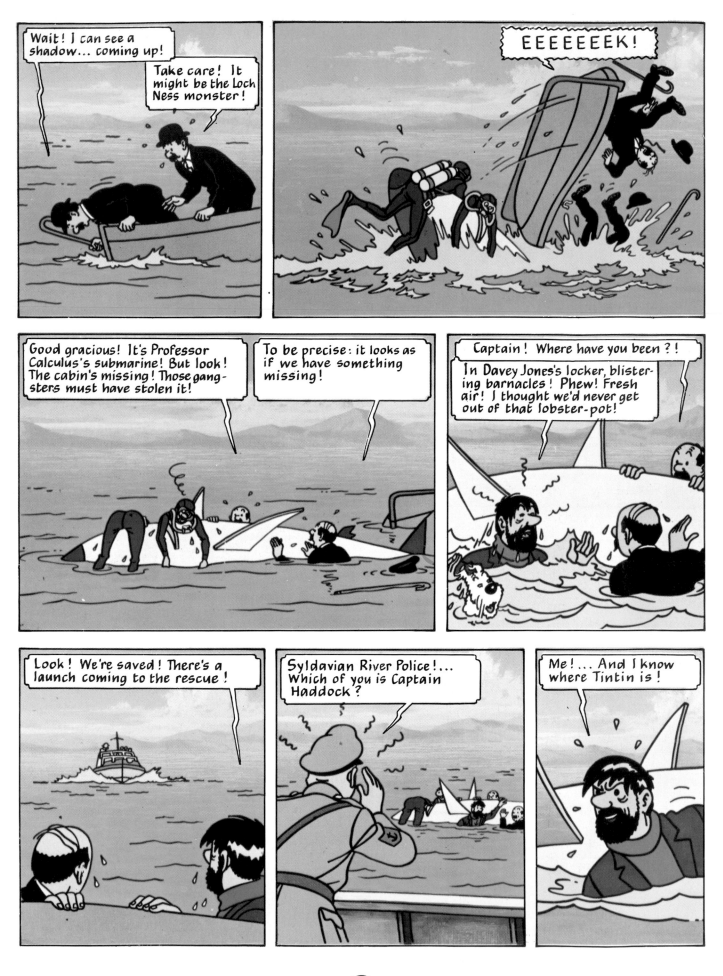

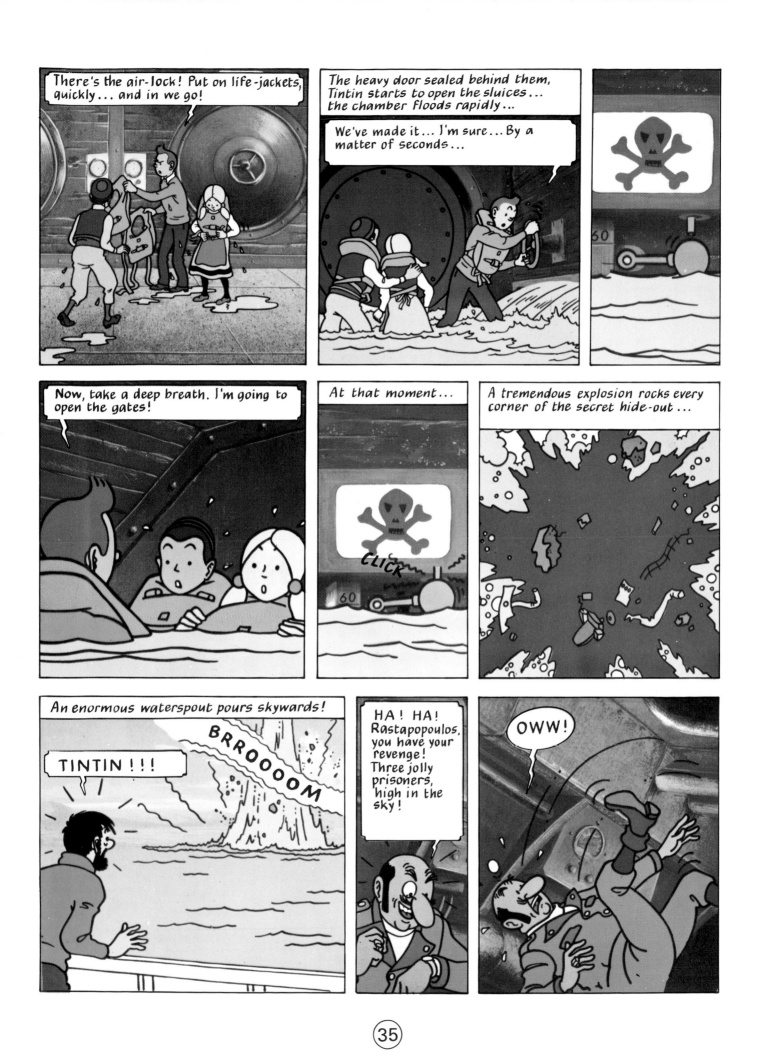

For what seems a lifetime, the tiny vessel is buried beneath the churning water ... then, miraculously, she shakes herself free.

Billions of blue blistering barnacles!

Ah, we're all washed up!

To be precise: we're a complete washout!

Niko!... Where is Niko?!

Here! And there's Tintin!

All present and correct, everybody?

Hey! Help us to open the door! It's jammed!

That's the inspector's voice.

Ready! All together now!

CRACK

What about Rastapopoulos and his pirates?

Rastapopoulos! So it was him! Unfortunately, we haven't managed to catch him yet...

... But at least we've picked up some of the sharks. One of our patrols fished out several handsome specimens, and another netted some more when they tried to dump their loot in a cave by the lake.

Inspector, sir! A radio signal!

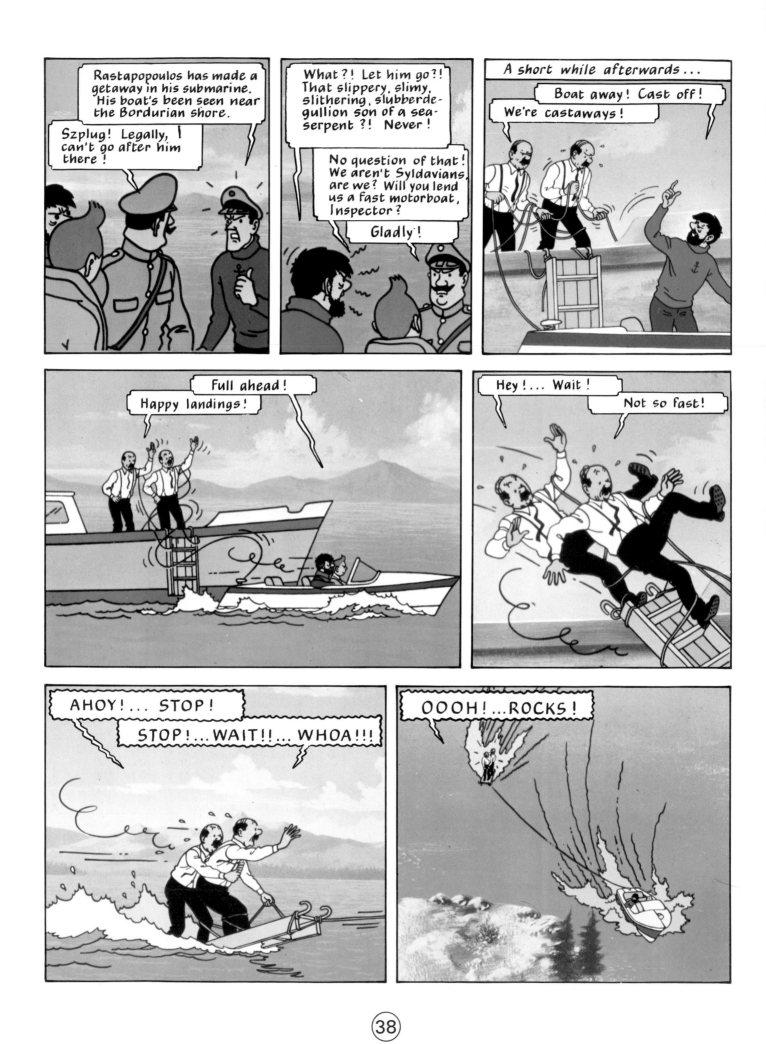

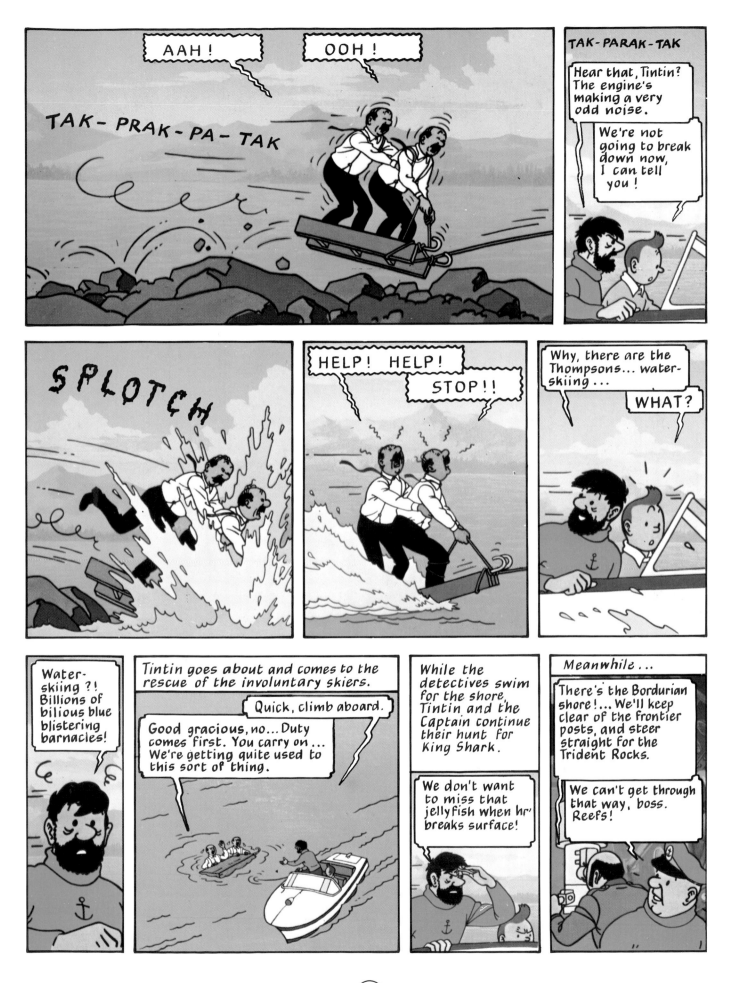